MW00935617

My Friend, Patricia

by

Avery Gordon

illustrated by
Mousam Banerjee

Copyright 2021 by Avery J. Gordon

All rights reserved. No part of this book may be

reproduced or used in any manner without written

permission of the copyright owner except for the use of

quotations in a book review.

All the illustrations are by Mousam Banerjee.

For Mom and Janine.
Thank you.

I have a friend Patricia,
who doesn't hear so well.

Sometimes I call her name,
and she doesn't answer me.

One day I asked my mommy,
" why when I call Patricia
she doesn't answer me?"

"Well Madison, Patricia is deaf."

"What is deaf Mommy?"

" When someone is deaf that means they cannot hear with their ears like us. They hear with their eyes."

" Hear with their eyes? That's silly Mommy."

"No, it's not silly. Deaf people hear differently than us. They use their hands to sign to one another, like how we use our mouths to talk."

"I will call Patricia's mom, so we can go over to her house, and we can learn about her culture."

Madison and Mommy
go to Patricia's house.

"Hello, Margarite!"
The mothers exchange pleasantries.

"Madison asked me why Patricia doesn't answer when she calls her name. I brought her over so she can learn how Patricia communicates."

"Oh, that is a lovely idea!
Come, she's in her room."

They walk to Patricia's room.

Patricia's back is to the door, so Ms. Margarite flashes the light on and off one time.

"Why did you do that?" Madison asked quizzically, "it's a way of getting Patricia's attention without scaring her."

Patricia turns around and runs over to her mom and waves to Madison and her mommy.

Madison yells loudly, "HELLO PATRICIA!"

Ms. Margarite chuckles, "you don't have to yell. She can't hear you. You can wave back, which means hello too."

Ms. Margarite begins to sign to Patricia while Madison is in awe.

"I want to learn!" exclaims Madison.

"Sure, here are the signs for asking to play. PLAY+WANT+YOU? Try it!"

Madison awkwardly signed
PLAY+WANT+YOU?

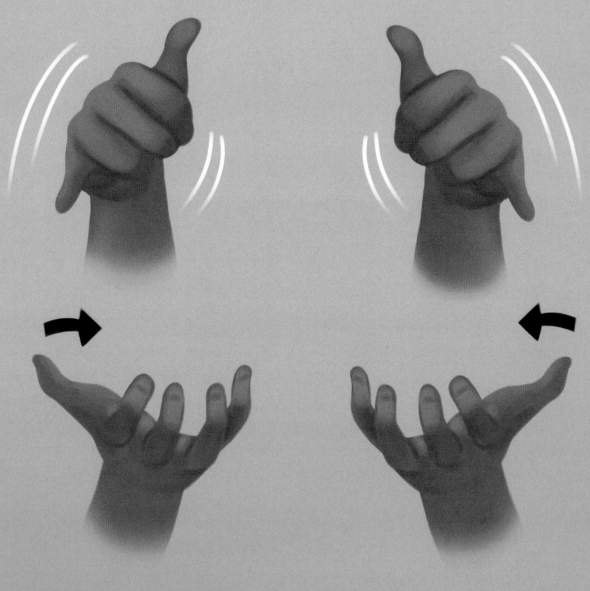

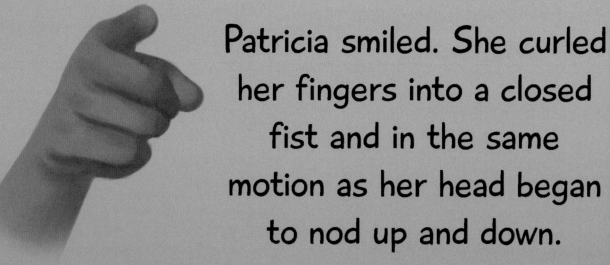

Patricia smiled. She curled her fingers into a closed fist and in the same motion as her head began to nod up and down.

"Why did Patricia shake her head and her fist?"
Ms. Margarite explained, "that means yes! Oh, we have so much to learn!"

The girls ran off to play.

The end!

About The Author

Avery Gordon is an entrepreneur with her Associates degree in American Sign Language English Interpreting. In addition she holds a certificate in Educational Interpreting. She has interpreted within several theaters such as The Brooklyn Academy of Music, Lincoln Center and The Apollo.

Made in the USA
Middletown, DE
15 April 2022

64304860R10020